This book has been presented to:

_____

And was first read to them by:

_____

The Reading Pig
Goes To School

Author—Nicholas I. Clement, Ed. D.

Illustrator—Judy Nostrant

Foreword—Emily L. Meschter, DHL

Teachers Change Brains Media books may be purchased for educational, business or sales promotional use.
For information – www.thereadingpig.com
Library of Congress Cataloging in Publication Data is available on request.

ISBN – 9780996389129 First edition. February 2016

Book management & marketing services – www.maxfemurmedia.com

Illustrations – Judy Nostrant

Cover layout & pre-press production — Pattie Copenhaver

Acknowledgements ~

Many thanks to these great people who came together
to bring the pig to life…….

Pima Federal Credit Union – Tucson, AZ
Thank you for your generous financial investment in
this project to benefit Children's Literacy programs.

Desert Lab Studio – Tucson, AZ
Thank you for your time and resource to share the
pig across the miles on *www.thereadingpig.com*

Northern Arizona University – Flagstaff, Arizona
Thank you to my colleagues across the College of Education
for their support in my endeavors as the
Ernest W. McFarland Citizens Chair in Education at NAU.

And to the countless others who cheered from the sidelines with
support and encouragement. Especially, Mr. Lyle Dunbar and his
staff and students at Richardson Elementary.

My gratitude, Nic

Anne Derrig,
your love of reading
lives on.

© 2016   Nicholas I. Clement
ISBN: 9780996389129
Published by:
Teachers Change Brains Media

www.legendaryteacher.com

A special foreword

from Emily L. Meschter, DHL

My dear friend, Nic Clement, is a retired public school superintendent who is still a teacher at heart and in spirit. He speaks and writes about education – eloquently, informatively, persistently, in all forms, at all levels, all the time. For over twenty years, I have heard and read his presentations. I am still in awe of his knowledge, his dedication and his respect for learning. His books are about teaching, his support and admiration of teachers, and his coaching of teachers. His audience is universal with a special emphasis on those who need to value teachers, not just value education. You are encouraged to support learning in all its many facets and venues.

It wasn't until the mid-1990s's that the U. S. Department of Education accepted that early childhood learning was not only possible but critically important. They finally began supporting professional teachers specializing in pre-kindergarten learning. Early literacy matters.

When you are an infant you are lucky that your mom or dad reads to you because you are learning to hear words and to recognize your parent's face and voice. You get cuddles and cooing and pictures to look at and recognize.

When you are one, you are really lucky that your parents read to you because you learn to associate sounds with facial expressions and familiar meanings and to make similar sounds yourself. You start to hold books and realize they contain stories and pictures for you to enjoy.

When you are two years old, you are really, really lucky that someone reads to you because you can see the words on a page and that they convey the story or poem you like. You start to say your own words, answer questions about the story, turn the pages, even ask your mom or dad to read it again, and again, and again because it is familiar and you like it a lot.

When you are three, you are really, really, really lucky that parents or other family members and baby-sitters read to you because you get to hear stories about wonderful people, fabulous places and interesting things. You may learn to recite whole phrases, detect rhyme and ask questions about what is going on in the book.

When you are four, you are really, really, really, really lucky because you can begin to read words in a book all by yourself, anytime, anywhere, for any reasons and enjoy the stories that go with the pictures. You may even read aloud to your cat or dog or your stuffed animal.

When you are five, you are really, really, really, really, really lucky to have all this reading experience because you have heard and learned the meaning of thousands more words than a child who has not been read to and usually hears only the word "no".

You are way ahead on your learning curve. Think about how much more you know, can learn, can do at five and for the rest of your life just because you were read to early on and learned to read by yourself.

Learning to read later is more difficult and so is teaching it. "The Reading Pig" tells such a story with humor without dismissing its importance. I hope all readers have a chance to enjoy the tale, reflect on its message, share the experience with others, and then take time to say "Thank-You" to a teacher.

Thank you, Nic.

Emily L. Meschter

Editor's note: *In 2012, Emily Meschter was awarded an Honorary Doctor of Humane Letters degree by the University of Arizona, College of Education for her long and distinguished career as a philanthropist and supporter of education.*

Enjoy the tale...

Hi, my name is Cole.

I want to tell you my story. One day we had a substitute teacher. His name was Dr. C. When we walked into our class, Dr. C was at the door. He was wearing a bright blue tie with funny shapes on it. He gave us all name tags with cool lanyards. The last time we got name tags, we went on a field trip to the zoo.

We saw elephants, tigers and bears.

We were *happy*.

We sat in our seats. We got very quiet. We could not wait to get in line for the bus. Then… he told us that we were not going on a field trip to the zoo.

We were *disappointed.*

Dr. C gave us name tags so he would
know our names.

Dr. C told us he was the superintendent.
He would be our substitute for the day.

We were *confused*!

I asked him what a superintendent did. Dr. C told us that his job was to help our principal and teachers teach us. Dr. C tried hard to cheer us up. He showed us a pig. He said it was his reading pig and we would use the reading pig during reading circle.

We were *excited*!

We first played a sticker game. Dr. C gave us animal stickers for working hard. We were thrilled. My first sticker was a monkey with long arms. Monkeys are my favorite. My sticker ripped and part of it got stuck to Dr. C's arm. He explained that we did not have time to finish the sticker game.

RRRip!

We were glum.

Dr. C looked at the clock.

He told us it was time to go to an assembly.

We had to explain to Dr. C about the line
leader and caboose

We were *helpful*.

After the assembly, we walked back to class.
On the way back, Amanda let me hold a box.
She told me that her tooth was in the box.

She brought it for show and tell.
It was show and tell time.

She was *happy*!

During Show and Tell, Dr. C dropped Amanda's tooth box on the floor. We all got on the floor to help her find her tooth.

She was *unhappy*!

We found Amanda's tooth!

Amanda went first for Show and Tell.

She was *overjoyed*!

Finally, it was reading circle time. Dr. C told us to sit on the floor. He sat in the reading chair and reached in his bag. He pulled out his reading pig.

We were *smiling*.

Dr. C held the reading pig up high. He told
us that it was a special reading pig.
The reading pig was squishy and had a
funny nose.

We were *laughing*.

Dr. C told us that at the end of each page we would pass the reading pig. I held the reading pig first. We couldn't wait for Dr. C to start reading. Dr. C gave me the reading pig. I hit it with my hand and it made a funny noise. It went WOP. I put the reading pig on the floor and hit it with both hands.

WOP, WOP, WOP!!!!

I was very *happy*!

Dr. C finished reading the first page. He asked me to pass the reading pig to Amanda. I didn't want to pass the reading pig. Dr. C pulled on the reading pig and I held on to the reading pig's leg. Dr. C pulled harder and I held on tighter. Dr. C pulled even harder and held on to both legs. Then, I let go. The reading pig went flying all the way across the room.

It was funny but Dr. C wasn't *smiling*!

Dr. C gave Amanda the reading pig.
She was very happy. After we all held the
reading pig which took a long time, we
asked to get a drink. Dr. C kept
telling us that we could get a
drink later.
We were thirsty.
When it was
time for library,
Dr. C looked very
happy. On the way
to the library, we
stopped and got a
drink. We all tried
to drink from the
same fountain at
the same time.
We were
crowded!

At the end of the day, Dr. C looked very tired. I asked him if he knew any magic tricks. He said yes and we all sat in our seats.

We were
fired up!

He took his reading pig and put it in a big hat. Dr. C told us to say the magic word "oink" three times.

We yelled, "Oink, Oink, Oink".

Dr. C turned the hat upside down and the reading pig was gone!

Dr. C put the hat on his head. He told us to say the magic words again. "Oink, Oink, Oink" He took his hat off. There it was sitting on his head, the reading pig.

We were *amazed*.

We now know what superintendents do. They help make reading fun by bringing their reading pig to school.

The end.

The Reading Pig – Vocabulary Activity

Read aloud some of the words from my story. Learn how to pronounce them and learn how to spell them. And, learn what they mean.

Happy   Helpful
Fired up
Disappointed   Amazed
Smiling   Confused
Excited
Laughing   Overjoyed
Unhappy
Crowded

…..and, just like me, read daily. Either by yourself or ask someone to read to you.

Enjoy!

Reed Daly - *The Reading Pig*

CPSIA information can be obtained
at www.ICGtesting.com
Printed in the USA
JSHW021157050521
14321JS00003B/37

9 780996 389129